Sprout, Seed, Sprout!

Owlkids Books acknowledges the financial support of the Canada Council for
the Arts, the Ontario Arts Council, the Government of Canada through the
Canada Book Fund (CBF) and the Government of Ontario through the Ontario
Media Development Corporation's Book Initiative for our publishing activities.

Published in Canada by
Owlkids Books Inc.
1 Eglinton Avenue East
Toronto, ON M4P 3A1

Published in the United States by
Owlkids Books Inc.
1700 Fourth Street
Berkeley, CA 94710

Library of Congress Control Number: 2018946400

Library and Archives Canada Cataloguing in Publication

Dunklee, Annika, 1965-, author
        Sprout, seed, sprout! / written by Annika Dunklee ; illustrated
by Carey Sookocheff.

ISBN 978-1-77147-308-8 (hardcover)
        I. Sookocheff, Carey, 1972-, illustrator II. Title.

PS8607.U542S67 2019   jC813'.6   C2018-903434-3

Edited by: Karen Boersma
Designed by: Alisa Baldwin

Manufactured in Dongguan, China, in September 2018,
by Toppan Leefung Packaging & Printing (Dongguan) Co., Ltd.
Job #BAYDC61

A   B   C   D   E   F

ONTARIO ARTS COUNCIL
CONSEIL DES ARTS DE L'ONTARIO
an Ontario government agency
un organisme du gouvernement de l'Ontario

Canada Council
for the Arts

Conseil des Arts
du Canada

Canadä

Publisher of Chirp, Chickadee and OWL
www.owlkidsbooks.com

Owlkids Books is a division of

Bayard
CANADA

To father — AD
To my brother Luke — CS

Sprout, Seed, Sprout!

Written by
Annika Dunklee

Illustrated by
Carey Sookocheff

Owlkids Books

One.

Two.

Threeeeee...

An avocado seed!

One
glass of water.

Two
careful hands.

Three
pointy toothpicks.

Poke.

Poke.

Poke.

Waiting.

Waiting.

Waiting!

Nothing.

Three heartfelt words:

"Sprout, seed, sprout!"

One root!

Two roots!

Three roots!

"YAY!"

One pot.

Two
careful hands.

Three scoops of soil.

Pat,
pat,
pat.

Three sprinkles of water.

Splish!
Splosh!
Splash!

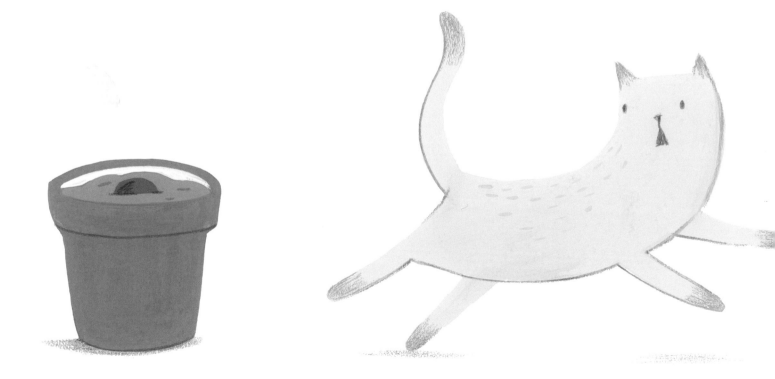

Sunshine.

Waiting.

Waiting.

Waiting!

Nothing.

Three drastic measures:

One
encouraging song.

Two
lucky coins.

Three
supportive
friends.

Waiting.

Waiting.

Waiting!

Still nothing.

Three frustrated words:

"I . . . GIVE . . . UP!"

One...   two...   three
                                                                      more days.

One sturdy stem.
Two clapping hands.
Three grateful cheers:

"HOORAY! HOORAY! HOORAY!"

One dug-out hole.

Two careful hands.

Three magic words:

One year.

Two years.

Three years.

One, two, three—an avocado tree!